(yellow)

Blue Is My Name!

by Angela C. Santomero
illustrated by Karen Craig

Ready-to-Read

Simon Spotlight/Nick Jr.

ew York   London   Toronto   Sydney   Singapore

NOTE TO PARENTS

Welcome to the first in a series of Ready-to-Read books done the Blue's Clue way! This line of books has been researched with preschoolers to ensure a high level of interactivity in this simple rebus format. Preschoolers are encouraged to read along with you by reading the pictures above the words in this story. Because the word is also underneath each picture, your preschooler will begin to recognize and learn each word as well! What's more, this line of books is reminiscent of Blue's journal. Each story has been written from Blue's own preschooler point of view and reveals her innermost feelings about the world around her.

To Traci Paige Johnson: Thank you for being a true visionary, a very best friend, and the cutest Blue puppy in the world. I look forward to the next ten years together!—A. C. S.

To my family—K. C.

Based on the TV series *Blue's Clues* ® created by Traci Paige Johnson, Todd Kessler, and Angela C. Santomero as seen on Nick Jr.®
On *Blue's Clues*, Steve is played by Steven Burns.

SIMON SPOTLIGHT
An imprint of Simon & Schuster Children's Publishing Division
1230 Avenue of the Americas, New York, New York 10020

Manufactured in the United States of America
First Edition   2 4 6 8 10 9 7 5 3 1

Library of Congress Cataloging-in-Publication Data
Santomero, Angela C.
Blue is my name / by Angela C. Santomero ; illustrated by Karen Craig. —
1st ed.
p. cm. — (Ready-to-read)
Based on the TV series Blue's clues created by Traci Paige Johnson, Todd Kessler,
and Angela C. Santomero as seen on Nick Jr.
Summary: Blue loves being blue because it is the color of the sky,
her favorite bird, water, and other wonderful things. Features rebuses.
ISBN 0-689-83122-6 (pbk.)
1. Rebuses. [1. Blue Fiction. 2. Rebuses.] I. Craig, Karen, ill.
II. Blue's clues (Television program) III. Title. IV. Series.
PZ7.S23825Bl 2000
[E]—dc21
99-16406

Hi, It's me,  BLUE !

I'm so HAPPY to see you.

3

4

is my name.
Do you know why?

BLUE

Because  is the BLUE color of the 🌥️🌥️ SKY .

6

BLUE is the color of my favorite **BIRD** in a **TREE**. The bird's **BLUE** like me, can you see?

8

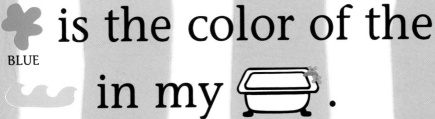 is the color of the in my .

BLUE

WATER

BATHTUB

BLUE is the color

of my TOWEL .

Rub! Rub! Rub!

12

Blue is the  that
I always choose,

CRAYON

15

when I write the number 2 2 2 .

TWO

 is also the color of my RAINHAT and 👟 !

BLUE

SHOES

is found in my
favorite .

PANCAKES

Just like the ones

MR. SALT

makes!

Shake! Shake! Shake

is my name.
I'm proud, don't
you see...

23

because  is
BLUE
the color of me!